The Jelly Bean Contest

The Jelly Bean Contest

By Kathy Darling

Drawings by Buck Brown

GARRARD PUBLISHING COMPANY
CHAMPAIGN, ILLINOIS

The Jelly Bean Contest

Teddy stuck his head
in the Jet's clubhouse.
He yelled, "Am I late?"
"No," said Chuck,
the leader of the Jets.
"I'm calling the roll."

"Jim," he called.

"Here," said Jim.

"Teddy," he called.

"Here," said Teddy.

"Oscar," he called.

"Here," said Oscar.

"Everybody is here," said Chuck.

"I'm here too," said Sammy.

He was Ben's little brother.

"You aren't a member,"
Chuck said.

"What are you doing here?"

"Mom made me bring him,"
said Ben.

Chuck looked at Sammy.

He made a mean face.

He said in a mean voice,

"All right, Mr. Tag-along,

you can stay today.

But you have to be quiet."

"Ben," Chuck said, "give us

the treasurer's report."

"We have $6.31," Ben said.

The boys wanted

to buy a football.

They started to talk about

ways they could earn money.

"I almost forgot!" Chuck said.

"The candy store has a sign

in the window.

It says:

JELLY BEAN CONTEST!
GUESS HOW MANY JELLY BEANS
ARE IN THE JAR.
THE CLOSEST NUMBER WINS.
FIRST PRIZE IS A FOOTBALL.
ONE GUESS ONLY.

"That's how we can get
a football," the boys shouted.
"Let's go," Jim said.
"Let's go win that football!"
He ran to the door.

Everybody pushed and shoved,
trying to get out.
Down Maple Street they ran.
Jim was in the lead.
The others were right behind.
"Wait for me," called Sammy.

"Wait for me. I want to count
the jelly beans too."
The others didn't wait.
The Jets lined up
in front of the candy store.

The jelly bean jar
was in the window.
So was the football.
It was the kind they wanted.
Jim whistled.
"It's a beauty," he said.
"It sure is," said Chuck,
"and it's going to be ours."
They all looked at the jar.
Sammy couldn't see.
He tried to wiggle
close to the window.
Ben shoved him away.
While the boys were looking,
some more boys
came down the street.

They were the Kings.
They wanted to win
the football too.
"Look who's here, boys,"
called Billy,
the leader of the Kings.

"You Maple Street Jets
might as well get lost.
The Kings are going to win
this contest," he shouted.
"My big brother
is going to help us."

"We don't need any help,"
Chuck shouted back.
"We can win it alone.
Just you wait and see."
The Kings walked
on down the street.
"Can you figure out
how many jelly beans
there are, Oscar?
You are the best in math,"
Chuck said.
Oscar looked at the jar.
He scratched his head.
He thought and thought.
Then he said,
"I have an idea.

Let's count
all the black ones
and then multiply
by the number of colors."
"That's a good idea,"
everyone cried.

They began to count
the black jelly beans.
They counted
the ones on the top.
They counted
the ones on the bottom.

They counted
the ones on the sides.
Sometimes they counted
a jelly bean twice.
They thought
that there were
200 black jelly beans.

"Now let's count the colors,"
Oscar said.
"I see pink ones
and white ones,"
called Teddy.
"There are two kinds
of blue ones," Ben added.

"Don't forget
the green ones," Oscar said.
"I won't forget
the green ones,"
Sammy told Oscar.
"I like them best.
They taste like limes."

"Be quiet! You'll get us
mixed up," Ben said
to his little brother.
They found seven colors.
Black made eight.

"Now Oscar
can do the math,"
Chuck said.
Oscar closed his eyes.
His lips moved.

"The answer is
1,600 jelly beans!"
he cried.
He ran into the store.
"I know how many jelly beans
there are in the jar.

The Jets are going
to win the football!"
Mrs. Winters said,
"Be careful.
You get only one guess."

"There are 1,600,"
Oscar said.
"I am sorry, Oscar.
You aren't even close,"
Mrs. Winters said.

"No one else
can guess now,"
said Chuck.
"We've got to think
of a new way
to guess the right number."
The Jets walked to the park.

They were quiet,
for they were all thinking.
They wanted very much
to win the football.
"I know why
that guess wasn't right,"
Oscar said.

"We didn't count
the jelly beans
in the middle."
"What we need," Chuck said,
"is a jar like the one
in the candy store.

Then we can count
those in the middle."
Sammy pulled Ben's shirt.
"Leave me alone,
you dumb little kid,"
said Ben.
"I'm trying to think."

"But, Ben,"
Sammy said again,
"mom has a jar
just like that."
They all ran to Ben's house.

His mother said
they could use the jar.
"We don't have
any jelly beans,"
said Jim.

"What can we
fill it with?"
"We can use rocks
the size of jelly beans,"
Teddy said.
"Our driveway
has lots of them."

They took the jar
to Teddy's driveway.
Everybody looked for rocks
the size of jelly beans.
Sammy got in the way.
He put a bug in the jar.

The boys yelled at him.
They made him sit
on the front steps.

The Jets counted
as they filled the jar.
Sometimes a boy
put in a big rock.
Sometimes he put in
one too small.

Some of the rocks
that were counted
fell in the grass.
Chuck did the counting.
When he got to 1,010,
the jar was full.
The boys were very tired.

"This has to be
the right answer," Chuck said.
"Come on, I'll race you
to the candy store.
I bet we win the football."
They ran back
to the candy store.

"I guess 1,010,"
Chuck said, breathless.
"We've had a closer guess,"
Mrs. Winters said.
"Who wants to try next?"
The boys stood around
the jar again.

"I have an idea," said Ben.
"May I pick up the jar?"
he asked Mrs. Winters.
"Yes, but don't drop it,"
she said.
"It weighs fifteen pounds,"
Ben said.
"I guess there are
15,000 jelly beans
in fifteen pounds."
"That's not right either,"
said Mrs. Winters.
"You other boys
will need to guess
before tomorrow afternoon,"
she added.

"It's the last day
of the contest."
Sadly the boys went home.
The next morning
Teddy called the other members.
"Meet me at the clubhouse,"
he said.

"I know how
to win the contest."
He told Ben
to bring the jar.
When the boys
got to the clubhouse,
Teddy was already there.

He had a big bag
of jelly beans
and a ruler.
"Watch while I measure
the jar," he said.
"It's ten inches high.
Now I'll add
one inch of jelly beans."

Happily the boys
counted the jelly beans.
But Ben didn't count
the red ones he ate.

When the boys were through,
they had counted
1,100 jelly beans.
"Now," said Teddy,
"1,100 times 10 is 11,000.
There are 11,000
jelly beans in the jar!"

The boys ran down
the street toward the store.
They saw the Kings
coming out the door.
The boys hurried
to look in the window.
The football was still there,
so they went inside.

"Hi, boys!" said Mrs. Winters.

"Do you have another guess?"

"Yes," said Teddy.

He told her his answer.

Mrs. Winters waited

for a minute,

and then she shook her head.

"You have used
your guess, Teddy,
and it's not close enough.
I'm sorry."
"It's my turn now,"
said Jim.

"The contest is almost over,
so I'll use
my lucky number.
It's 25.
I guess 25 hundred jelly beans!"
"That's not lucky enough
to win a football,"
Mrs. Winters said.

The Jets were sad.
They had used
all their guesses.
Now they couldn't
win the football.
They started to leave.

"Wait," said Sammy.
"I haven't guessed yet.
I guess 1-2-3-4-5 because
that's the biggest number
I know."

The Jets laughed.
"What a stupid guess,"
they cried.
"Sammy can't win.
He can't even count!"

But Mrs. Winters was smiling.
She went to the window
and picked up the football.

"Surprise!" she said to Sammy.
"Your guess is the closest.
The contest is over,
and you are the winner!

The football is yours!"
She handed the football
to Sammy.

He took the football
and smiled at Mrs. Winters.
"Thank you very much,"
he said to her.
The Jets cheered.

"Hooray for Sammy!"
they cried.
They patted him
on the back.

"Sammy, would you like
to join the Jets?"
Chuck asked.
"We can have a quick vote,"
Teddy added.

"Sure, we want Sammy
to be a Jet,"
all the boys shouted.

"I don't know,"
said Sammy.
"I might join the Kings."
He walked down the street
tossing his new ball
in the air.

The other boys followed him.
"Can we play
with your new ball?"
the Jets asked.
"Sure," said Sammy,
"if I can be
the next leader
of the Jets!"